BITTERS

BITTERS

Kaaron Warren

CEMETERY DANCE PUBLICATIONS

Baltimore

❖ 2023 ❖

Cemetery Dance Publications
132B Industry Lane, Unit #7
Forest Hill, MD 21050
www.cemeterydance.com

Trade Paperback Edition

ISBN:
978-1-58767-870-7

An hour it took McNubbin to drive to work and the stink of the Man with him all the way. What he did was listen to the audio book of his wife reading "History of the Man". She did it for him and no one else. Her love letter to him, her voice all soft and sexy. She made the recordings when they were early together, and still the words brought back to him those hot days when they were fit and young and carefree.

"He's got all his limbs, this huge metal man, and we know he's a man because he's got that, too, stiff and long, halfway down his thigh, semi-erect and always that way," her voice all breathy.

"Three men, arms stretched, can only just touch fingers around one shin. You'd have to stand sixty men tall to reach his head if there weren't the steps winding around. His arms are crossed over his chest, as if he is hugging himself, and one finger pokes out, admonishing us all to behave.

"The metal is copper-colored but not copper, some substance long since exhausted, the last of it melted to forge this giant.

"He's been here well beyond living memory, more than a thousand years. It took a hundred years to build him, section by section, the workmanship so perfect that if you ran your fingers over the joins you could only feel a slight ridge.

"The first bodies went in while he was still being polished."

The eleventh broken girl was so fresh dead McNubbin could feel the last of her pulse, he thought. Could feel the blood flowing although nothing else was there.

He carried her up the 400 steps to the Man's mouth, sad for her strength and future, love and all ahead of her, and later said to his workmates, *where are they coming from? These broken girls?* They all had the required ID, the approvals, the medical proof of drug-free, yet none were local. Locals weren't flawed. These ones had skin blemishes, cloudy eyes. You could tell they hadn't taken bitters all their lives.

Who was breaking them?

Mostly McNubbin didn't question who he carried up to the Man's mouth. The only rule was they had to carry the bodies to the Man within three days. Sooner the better, freshest best. It was not their business who was who; not theirs to decide, although carriers were trained to smell the wrong ones, those too long dead, or preserved, or filled with drugs. They didn't go into the Man. People didn't realise how skilled the carriers were. Jervis, a carrier long ago gone missing, had been a stickler for it. The bodies he rejected! Thing was, he was always right, and when he said no, all of them refused. It wasn't that they didn't sneak some in, but mostly the sneaky ones came from the professors, tweaks to the Bitters. The carriers would never put the Bitters at risk. Jervis thought he knew better than the professors, better than their supervisor, Orton, better than the other carriers. He knew how to say no, that's for sure. That was a man barely missed; a loner, no friends, no family. McNubbin did wonder sometimes why he ran off, considering his obsession for the job and nothing else in his life. But each to their own and his not to judge.

The eleventh broken girl seemed to shift and he imagined, as he sometimes did with the nice ones, that she was still alive. He imagined carrying her back down and keeping her safe in his small house, making her soup and she would rub his feet for him with her thin, cold fingers. His wife wouldn't mind. Her fingers were old and tired and well past rubbing.

McNubbin started carrying at 14, one of the youngest and he was proud of that. He felt every step now, 32 years later, but still he climbed steadily. You had to take each step on its own merit. They were well-maintained, serviced every single night, but even so, fluids dripped, thick and slippery. You had to watch your footing. A fall could break all your limbs, and had. McNubbin's brother had tripped over and fallen headtoeheadtoeheadtoehead to the ground. They had to scoop him up in order to carry him back to the top and that was McNubbin's job. Much as it still gave him nightmares, it was no one else's place but his to tip his own brother in.

No one else's place to tell his widow, too, and whisper it over the head of his tiny baby girl and tell lies to his son, four years old and not so bright.

The girl's breasts pressed into his back as he carried her slung that way, and her thighs under his fingers felt both soft and firm.

Step by step, he reached the top. The smell was far worse up there and you had to be careful, because your eyes might tear up and your head spin no matter how used to it you were. It was a chemical thing, they'd been told in training. You did not want to be dizzy at the top.

His head was the only open part of him and that hole, right at the top and angled for access, was big enough to take the bodies. His head tilted back at an angle that would hurt a real man, his mouth wide open. No teeth. More than once fat men have been sliced in two to fit. Children slipped in easy, as if on a fun ride.

Women bent more going in and no one had the answer as to why.

Quickly now, no longer enjoying the feel of the woman's body, McNubbin propped her against the metal Head, reached over to the knife rack and selected his favourite, a medium-sized blade. He drew it quickly across her jugular, making sure she was dead before tipping her expertly into the mouth hole. It was a nightmare they all shared, the idea of ending up in the Man still alive, so this final slash was another job the carriers had to do. Regardless of the cause of death, they slit the throats.

He heard the broken girl fall, passing through the broad throat, onto the breast bone, and *thud* into the chest area.

He waited for a moment, his head tilted sideways. Listening for the faint gurgle, the sound of shifting, as she sank. He liked to hear it; it meant the job was complete.

BITTERS

McNubbin carefully made his way back down. Down was good, though hard on the knees. Down meant you were on your way to the break room where you could eat, if your stomach was up to it, or talk, or sleep. He looked forward to seeing Swain and Clive, his usual workmates, who'd be ready with a cup of tea and a good joke for him.

There was no room on the steps to pass. One climbed, one rested, one prepared. The two not climbing could talk and cook meals in the break room, and ready jokes for the climber.

On shift, they were allocated an hour to walk up, twenty minutes for disposal and rest, thirty minutes to climb down. Some climbed quickly to give themselves spare minutes up there to contemplate.

At the bottom, he nodded at the salter who was ready to make his way up with his big bag. The salt wasn't as heavy as the bodies, and it didn't smell or leak, but the bags were unwieldy and hard to carry. Some salters were women, those women who'd built their muscles to do it. Why not? There weren't many. And there were no women carriers.

Squatting at the Giant's feet, a toe-tapper was at work. Dozens of tiny clear bottles sat beside her on the workbench. McNubbin watched as she turned the tap plugged into His enormous big toe and held a bottle underneath to catch a drop of the dark brown, viscous liquid that oozed from the tap.

It was a beautiful thing. McNubbin reached out to catch the last small drop, which he rubbed on his gums. She tutted but only in an habitual way. They all took the drops.

McNubbin had wanted to be a toe-tapper but his fingers were too thick and clumsy, even at 14. He would have been the first of them in the family. His brother preferred to be a carrier, even as a kid that's what he wanted. He was singleminded about it, and you'd think he would have been a natural. Strong enough. But no concentration. That's what got him. He was always easy to distract as a child. McNubbin had stolen many a cake from him by pointing out a bird or a bright car in the distance.

Their sister never wanted to be a toe-tapper, even though she had the fingers for it. Squatters, she used to call them. *Sitting on their haunches all day. Who'd do it*, she said. And she was a lost case by the time she was sixteen, given to drugs, and that broke all their hearts. Even if she threw it off, cleaned herself up, she wouldn't be allowed to serve Him, nor would she go into the Man when she died. It brought shame on the McNubbin family who were generations serving, but at least they had the reputation of the past, and he and his brother served well.

Toe-tappers had a gentleness about them, a softness of face. They weren't supposed to use the bitters any more than the recommended dosage, but there was always spillage and none of it should go to waste. His wife had been one for a while and she hadn't yet lost that softness.

"It's running slow today," the toe-tapper said. Thelma worked methodically, without fuss. McNubbin and his wife had known Thelma all their lives, just about. Wanda and Thelma had worked together early on, before Wanda's back turned bad and she had to give up toetapping.

"Weather's cold."

"Won't stop them coming in droves." The annual Hundred Year Day was coming up and the population would triple. They'd all be busy.

"They'll appreciate the chilly weather." In the hot weather the Giant's stench reached as far as McNubbin's house. They'd have to sit inside, most days. If there was ever a time people left, it was in the height of summer.

"Who've you tipped in today?" Thelma asked him.

"Young woman, car accident looked like. That's how broken she was. And a man died of heart disease." A good carrier could tell by the feel and the look what death it was, even without the papers.

The toe-tapper nodded. "There's a lot going in with the heart. That'll bode well, hundred years from now." They all liked to think they understood the bitters, could estimate what would come out even though it was the professors and their papers up at the school who made the decisions. McNubbin's head spun with it all. It was like travelling forward in time and what they did affected the future but by the time the future came the past would be gone and the future they were looking at was decided by the past and that's when his head spun.

His daughter was up at the University now and he couldn't be prouder, even if he didn't understand one tenth of the words she said these days. It was important work up there, analyzing the bitters, making adjustments for the future. It hadn't changed her at all. She was still his tough cookie, his heart of gold, his tower of strength. Like mother like daughter.

Thelma said, "Tell Wanda I tapped a special bottle for her. Batch 6292. See if she can order it in."

This was a private toe-tappers' joke. He wasn't sure what was funny about it, but Wanda would.

He pushed his way through the addicts lolling around the base wall, built to keep them and others out. There were always three or four of them and no matter how many complaints were made, how many times they were jailed for loitering, still they came back. Even the smell of the Man could make them high, they had so much juice in their blood. And they hung about hoping for a lick they never got. You knew which ones were addicts. Long term over-use did damage and made changes to the body, and these people had the classic too-soft features, the hair that sat thin and close to their scalps, the fingernails short, below the quick. If they restricted their addiction to the bitters they'd still be welcome in the Man and that seemed to give them comfort. They made McNubbin feel itchy and he wished they weren't there. At least his sister was elsewhere; when she hung around he wised he was blind, deaf and dumb so he didn't know she was there, shaming him.

Swain passed McNubbin, starting on his carry. They nodded at each other, winked. Everybody liked Swain better than his predecessor Jervis, that obsessive, rule-driven man who'd thrived on catching people out.

"Baby out yet?" McNubbin asked.

"Any day now," Swain said.

McNubbin headed to the tearoom where Clive was buttering a sweet bun.

"High Tea, your Highness?" McNubbin said.

"You call this High Tea? In a ROYAL household this is considered horse fodder." Clive sniffed his nose in the air in the way he did, a joke so old and familiar it was mostly said for comfort.

"I just carried up another broken girl," McNubbin said.

"I did two yesterday," Clive said. "Security guards from the Uni brought them in."

For the extras, the favours they did for the professors (as approved by Orton) they moved more quickly, needing it done before anyone noticed, so your legs would work like pistons, up and down, and you'd take less care. McNubbin had been carrying special choices for a long time. *Slip this one in*, Orton would say, and the supervisors before him as well.

Usually they were bodies of out-of-state. Murder victims, perhaps. They were people the professors thought needed to go in but were possibly not On The Books, not in an official way. Mostly they were brought in by security guards from the University, men who took no argument because they weren't interested.

They all took up the occasional body not on the official list, and that was something they kept to themselves. It made them feel lesser men, that not one of them would stand up and say no. But they never put bodies in if they'd be bad for the bitters. They trusted that the professors wouldn't send any wrong ones, but that every body was carefully selected for cause of death. The broken girls weren't wrong, not like that. They'd make nice juice in the Man. But they'd died wrong, was the thing.

"Should we tell someone?" Clive said.

Did it matter? All die in the end; all are bitters. But McNubbin had a daughter around the age of the broken girl he'd carried, and he couldn't help thinking it could have been a friend of hers, might be her one day.

"We should let Orton know, at least. That we think there are too many coming in."

"You better do that. He's scared of me," Clive said. They smiled at each other; Orton was scared of no one, least of all Clive, who was mild and short-boned. People said Clive and his family were in-bred. He said they were well-bred. They believed they were descended from royalty, as it existed before the Man, and that they needed to keep the line clear for the time when kings and queens were wanted again.

Clive didn't care so much for that, but he loved to joke about it.

McNubbin and Orton had known each other since children; sometimes McNubbin had to remind himself to treat the man like a boss, not like the kid he once was.

He found Orton in Packaging, having a go at the manager there. Orton was always on the go, always moving. He liked to be in motion.

McNubbin walked with him, talking quickly, about the broken girls (at least 11, he said, although there could be more) all of them with proper papers that could well be faked, and all of them about an age.

"Thing is, Orton, it could be my daughter and that hits home. These girls are dying nasty and they shouldn't be. We need to find out where they're coming from."

Orton kept walking but he turned and made like a crab, sideways, so he could look at McNubbin when he spoke.

"It could have been your sister, once upon a time, given the company she kept. After we broke up, of course." There was a time when Orton might have been a brother-in-law, but that was before she turned to drugs. She had lots of friends then. These days she kept no company at all, hiding away in a room on the other side of the country, pretending she didn't care about the Man or anything else.

She'd be buried, or left for the birds. Or sent away in a refrigerated truck somewhere else. Wasn't their business. She'd been an active little girl but now, any photos she sent showed her spilling over a large armchair, her facial features lost in flesh.

"So maybe you need to think about that. Your sister and how you could have saved her. That's maybe what you're worried about, McNubbin. Leave the planning to the Professors."

McNubbin took one more carry, slowly, letting the steps talk to him. This one was an older lady, someone's mother, and she'd had a good life from the flesh on her and the tightness of the skin on her face. No scars. He liked these carries; there was a sense of rightness about them. A sense of completion.

McNubbin liked to think as he carried. It was a time for contemplation, with no one at him, no family member needing a hug, no nephew needing to be driven somewhere, no daughter wanting advice. Of course, what he mostly thought about was his loved ones, but in his mind they were all sorted, and he could play over the good moments. The laughs and the times he and his wife fell in love again and again.

He barely noticed the smell of the Man anymore. Those born close by grew with it as part of their consciousness, they were used to it and in fact found the air elsewhere harsh and thin, but visitors described it as an ancient tin of sardines. Those who left were made homesick by the smell of fish paste. They took supplies of bitters with them but perhaps it was the smell of the Man himself that carried protection? Because often they would sicken, and it would be years before they were strong again after they came back.

The sensible people didn't leave.

For some, even a day away was enough to clear the nostrils and make coming back difficult. Those who left and returned bought incense by the truckload and it burnt in every room of their homes. Those who never left needed no such thing.

McNubbin had never left; what for? He liked his work as carrier, was paid far more than any other labourer, more than the teachers, more even than the ones who went away to University, whose noses cleared and who did jobs McNubbin could barely imagine.

This was the best career option. You went into the job straight out of school, no matter what age or academic achievement.

All you needed was a strong back and a strong stomach.

BITTERS

When he was new to it, McNubbin had tried to put it about a lot. He was young and new to carrying and naively thought people would love him for it. Girls. Plenty of money coming in, not much going out, so he had it to spend. To waste, his father said, but the old man was nothing but a shopkeeper, selling groceries as if he was anywhere in the world. That was the waste. McNubbin spent his school years working there in the afternoon, enough to be sure that was not the life he wanted. His father loved it. The customers, and the product. He loved unpacking a box of tins or a box of boxes. McNubbin found it sad to watch; the shallowness of it. His mother worked there too but she didn't love it much.

If ever he tired of carrying he thought of those fussy customers, spending a small amount but expecting a lot of attention, and he knew he'd made the right choice.

When he was new to it, McNubbin would boast to the ladies about what he did. They recoiled. Time after time, he could almost see their flesh creep.

It made him angry; made all of the carriers angry. "They are here because of us! This town would be nothing but burial mounds." This was McNubbin, one night, rejected, drinking with the crew.

"And poor," from a toe-tapper.

"Stupid to hate where the wealth comes from."

Another round ordered. Bitters on the rocks or mixed with vodka. Such a mix is frowned upon by the dullards, but what better way to take your medicine? He remembered this night because it was when he'd met his wife. He'd nudged the others when she walked in but he was the only one who fell in love at first sight. She was tall, strong-looking, delicate-featured. Her hair around her head cut short, and he'd learn before long that she didn't like things around her face. She didn't like to be bothered. She had a sharp sense of humour and he loved to laugh and they spent hours that night talking. He thought of this, sometimes, as they sat together in their garden. She still made him laugh; he never regretted the courage it took to talk to her that night.

She'd laughed at him. "You walk past me half your shifts, you know, and never glance my way."

He'd looked at her harder and realized he did know her face. She worked at the toes of the Man, but McNubbin was so focused back then he barely noticed anything except the bodies he carried.

Back in the break room, Clive was stood, reading the paper, not really reading it but flicking through it. Sometimes they arrived together; sometimes Clive got there early. He wasn't happy at home like McNubbin was and he came to work to escape. He was sleeping with one of the entomologists and they liked to stay together near the Man. The entomologist kept track of the insects, bringing them up in jars if the numbers were down. The good insect people could tell by the buzz what was required; the others would stick their heads inside, or tap on the side of the giant. They'd take samples if they could, and check the bitters, though most people thought this last was just an excuse for a free sip. McNubbin had seen a thousand bugs go up in the last few days, due to the busy time. Body, salt, bugs. Body, salt, bugs. Clive watched her up and down and took her refreshments. McNubbin didn't want to know.

McNubbin never said anything. He didn't even tell his wife, although he felt guilty about that.

"Swain!" Clive said as McNubbin walked in.

McNubbin laughed. "You're not the brightest spark but you surely can tell the two of us apart!"

Clive laughed back at him, a man always full of good humour.

"No, it's his wife. The baby's coming!" Swain was a young man with a life ahead of him.

"Good luck to her and him," he said, and they drank a beer in honour of their workmate. Usually they'd wait till all three were done.

"I'll toss you for his last carry up," McNubbin said. McNubbin got it so he did that then headed for the showers.

He used the back of a knife to scrape off some of the sediment from his skin and wipe it into a small bottle. He would sell it, one day, along with all the others he'd filled. He considered it his extra pension. Dozens of little bottles, waiting for the day they needed a windfall. He knew he'd find a buyer; he'd been followed for what sat on his skin. People begged him, *let me suck your cock, your fingers, let me lick your neck*. This woman all skinny and stained and it wasn't his fault her mother had failed to nurture her, begging him to let her suck his body parts.

He showered. They provided very hot water, new scrubbing brushes daily, a variety of soaps. No one would say the workers weren't cared for.

Driving to collect his wife from her job at the archives, he listened to her audio book.

"*Dead stripped and gently washed. Naked I come into the world. And naked do I go.*

"*This is history and history is hard because it keeps on changing. Word of mouth says this and this and this but the people don't always listen. They'll change the way a story is told. But this is how it is.*

"*300 years ago, the town was going through a time of good health. People living long and hearty and the Man rang hollow, close to empty. We didn't know then what we know now, but we knew the Man needed filling.*

"*A series of graveyards were dug up. What payment was made is unknown, but money surely changed hands in exchange for the bodies. All well and good, and the Man started to fill.*

"*We didn't know them. Most of the bodies had been preserved, even though the rot had set in on some. Many were so well-preserved they sat like raw dough in the Man for the longest time.*"

He parked in front of the Archives. He still felt as if he was covered with a film of filth. He noticed it more when he came to this place, because the Archives building was all white and inside it smelt of lemons. It was always calm and sleepy there.

There were no beggars at the Archives, no addicts. Just citizens queuing to have their papers updated. He tried to remember the joke he was supposed to tell Wanda. He wished he'd written it down.

He leaned on his car, people watching, his arms dropped by his side. Sometimes it was all he could do to keep them lifted. He'd ask Wanda to drive home; the exhaustion had hit him. That last carry, the one he took for Swain, had done him in.

Wanda came down the stairs arm in arm with another woman. She was Felicity, he thought, although he never could keep track of all her friends. Wanda was the type who kept in touch with almost everybody she ever met and was always there for them to lean on. Sometimes he wondered if her deep-seated sadness came from this, that she absorbed all the troubles of others and they sat there like a cancer inside her.

The two women kissed cheeks. McNubbin waved and the friend waved back, but he thought she turned her nose up at him. Certainly she didn't come up and say hello.

Wanda hugged him hard, put her head on his chest. Took the keys without speaking and opened the door for him to climb in.

Wanda smelt of dust at the end of the day, and her fingers were calloused from all the files. She used to have the softest fingers when she was a toe-tapper. He'd loved that time. She'd always give him a smile when he came down, and a wink, and he felt such a sense of satisfaction, of a life well sorted, on seeing her there. Even after she changed jobs, she never commented on his smell. Because it got in the pores and there was no denying. You smelt like the Man even after a dozen showers. You went to your death smelling that way. She'd left after an accident, when her back ached her so much she couldn't bend to the toe. The Archives paid well but not as much and her back hurt her at this work as well.

She had no sense of smell, it turned out. Meant she didn't much care to eat, meant she was skinny. Meant she didn't smell him and he didn't smell himself so they were happy like that.

"I'm so exhausted," was the first thing she said. "I can hardly remember to breathe," with him stood there, an ache in every last muscle. He started the car; no question of who'd drive, then.

Around and about, the streets teemed with people caught up in their dramas and their joys. So many to keep track of. So many to record. Really, Wanda did work far harder than he did. He couldn't argue with that. Keeping the records straight and up to date took concentration, if not physical strain.

They kept both electronic and physical records. No one had faith in the computer records, and each person must have an up to date copy of their own files. Outsiders brought in to be added to the mix must come with such files; they needed a full record of drug use, for example. A full record of immunization and, in many cases, a summary of the standard diet. The town banned all preservatives in food, because they wanted no local to be refused. Outsiders were blood-tested and they would be refused if lies were discovered.

~

"How was the Man today?" she asked, as if he was a friend she no longer saw, and missed.

"Seemed a little peevish," he said, a joke they'd kept going for most of their marriage. "It's odd, though. We're getting in these girls…"

"Hmmm," she said.

"Nothing bad on me!" he said. "But they don't seem right. It seems as if someone is hurting them bad before they die. We don't like it. I told Orton about it but he didn't care much."

He didn't usually mention Orton around his wife. She didn't like him much.

"You should tell someone else," she said. "Give me their names, anyway, and I'll run a check at work."

"Hey," he said. "Thelma told me to give you a message but I can't remember it. It was a joke for you."

She smiled at him. "I'll call her later and she can tell me in person."

She filled him in, as she always did, about what she'd learned in the files that day. The illnesses, the deaths, the details of people's lives that only she would see, and that she would never see again once they were filed.

She sighed.

"I wish you wouldn't take it to heart so," he said. If he could get her away from the place he would, but he knew she'd only find the same unhappiness elsewhere.

"It's the inevitability of it all. The sameness."

"But at least we have a purpose. At least we're not going to waste."

She smiled at him then, and patted his hand. He grasped her fingers and drove one-handedly until he had to brake suddenly for traffic.

"Much as I love Hundred Year Day, I hate it, too," she said. "Year in year out in out in out, the crowding. All these strangers. Can't they just wait at home for their bitters to be delivered?"

He hated that the day made her sad. He loved this time of year, because of the buzz, the excitement, the new people in town. He loved the vendors lining the streets, selling food and other wares that would be otherwise unavailable. He loved the urgency of his job, the importance of it. If he were so inclined, he would be having sex on an hourly basis with grateful people. He had no desire for anyone but Wanda, though.

It wasn't just the sex lives of the single (and not so single) that were helped by the influx of visitors, and the economy. The professors were happy too because they knew there would be at least a couple of deaths and new blood was good for the Man, as long as it passed the test. It meant great glory for those strangers, which they would otherwise not have received.

~

He twisted the music dial (she hated listening to herself) to the station broadcasting non-stop readings, people with beautiful, somber voices listing all those who had gone into the Man and their cause of death. Nobody listened carefully, but you could tune in and tune out when you wanted. McNubbin found the readings calming and thought that others did, too.

They needed the calm; throughout the town, people were frantic knowing that a huge influx was coming. Demand would increase for the bitters and the toe-tappers worked 24 hours a day, filling the bottles to make sure there was enough. There were riots when there weren't enough bitters to sell and nobody wanted that again. The clean-up was disgusting when strangers bled all over the streets.

As well as the standard bottles, the toe-tappers filled commemorative statues, whose heads twisted off to be filled with the bitters. These cost ten times more, twenty times more, depending on demand. They were a chance to take the Man home because the statues were a perfect replica, swinging cock, arms crossed, pointing finger, all.

Most parents bought their children one at birth and perhaps one each year, depending on finances. McNubbin and his wife had just the two kids and they earned enough, so they had a good collection. They bought them for his sister's children, too. Why should they miss out?

They treasured the day each year when they would gather together and hand over the next statues. Their son and daughter still enjoyed it, even though they may be grown.

He dropped Wanda at their house then drove to pick up some groceries. He took a sneaky drink while he was at it; he deserved that.

Once home again, he parked on the street and walked down the side of his house to his mother's Granny Flat. He'd promised her to hang some pictures and he wanted to do it first, before dinner. After dinner he would sit in his chair and sleep. His wife would place a blanket on his lap and look fondly on him. Sometimes he woke up and saw her there, just looking at him, asleep with her eyes open. Inside, the house glowed with warmth and words.

No answer at the granny flat where his mother and two of the grandchildren stayed. He felt irritated but was calm by the time he entered his house. Of course they were all together inside.

McNubbin had tipped his own father into the Man. Not everyone liked to carry their own loved ones, but to many of them, it was a chance to say goodbye. You talked all the way up. Telling them the things you wanted them to know. Or you were silent in your thoughts, your memories. You knew you were doing great glory to them. Because there is glory in going into the Man. Your name remembered, recorded for all time.

McNubbin's father had died suddenly but without fear. Didn't know what hit him, they said. McNubbin always said he could tell the difference. Those who had died in fear had tighter muscles, for sure. Those who died peacefully had slack, soft muscles. His father had the latter and for that McNubbin was always thankful. He'd told his mother and she was happy, too. He'd said the same thing to Orton six months earlier and for once Orton had listened.

His grandfather was visiting, and his wife's too. His sister's kids, his own, and his brother's widow and their almost grown girl, all there for the Hundred Year Day celebrations. All of them sitting close together and the room felt warm. They cheered when they saw him.

"Who deserves a present?" he said. He always brought home treats of one kind or another. Today, he'd bought round sweets made from milk and dripping with honey. He handed them around. His mother said, "Before dinner!" but she happily ate hers and also one of the grandson's. This was McNubbin's sister's boy, born when she was deep in the throes of many addictions. His birth was one of the reasons she'd left. She wanted to get away from the bitters, as if that would help. Now she sought a different kind of drug, and not one that was good for her.

He'd never be okay, but he was a sweet, if irritating young man. Sometimes McNubbin thought that at least he'd contribute at the end of his life, by going into the Man, if he contributed nothing else.

"How is the Man?" his grandfather asked. None of them had the day to day interaction he had, and they all loved to hear the details.

"Working overtime!" McNubbin said, and they loved that joke.

They all pitched in, setting the table and bringing the food. Wanda stood there surveying the feast she'd risen at dawn to prepare but would eat very little of. McNubbin kissed her in gratitude. The love she showed in providing food she didn't like overwhelmed him, but there was some sorrow, too. He knew she overcompensated like this because otherwise she felt empty and lost.

He told his family about Swain's wife having the baby. "He didn't finish his shift, but no one expects you to concentrate with a baby coming."

"You don't need concentration to tell your legs to walk," Wanda said. She had a headache leftover from the day, working with the files. Sometimes being in the kitchen would ease it, but not today. McNubbin gave her temples a rub and she leaned into him gratefully. He loved how smart she was; how she could look at a room full of papers and know where they all should go. McNubbin never thought of himself as a smart person and he was glad about that. Smart made people unhappy and you didn't need it for what he did. But he didn't like it when she said they didn't have to think at all on the job.

"You should try it sometime. You can fall in if you don't concentrate," McNubbin told her, too weary to fight hard. "Don't forget about Timothy Hanlon." They all knew of the carrier who'd fallen in alive. Even saying his name gave McNubbin the chills. No one could imagine a worse death. It was an hour before anyone realized Hanlon had not walked down, and by the time two medics reached the top, he'd been in there at least two. They could still hear a faint call, but he was sunk deep down and no hook could reach him and there was no one who would go down after him.

Since Tommy Hanlon, all carriers and salters stitched a poison pill in the pocket of their work jacket, safe so the kids couldn't get to it by mistake.

Since then, suicide amongst carriers and salters had risen. Most would do it at the foot of the Man. Most suicides of any kind did that. Even in the depths of despair they didn't want to become waste. Fresh is best, and all you had to do was pick them up and carry them, once the professors had tested and approved.

Fresh was best. They would never put a preserved person in. Even a frozen one could affect the bitters and that was not on. So those who thought they could ship a loved one in from afar found the answer was no.

Timothy Hanlon went in only a year before McNubbin joined up at 14, so he was one of the first to take part in the new training. To make sure they never lost focus at the top, they simulated going into the Man. A large tub filled with rejected bodies and in they went for two minutes is all.

They did not have to strip naked for the training, although standing in underwear was bad enough.

McNubbin had called out, "But if we fall in, we'll be clothed, won't we? On the job?"

He didn't do it to be smart, but he did like the nudges his classmates gave. He was only 14 then; he could barely remember being that cocky.

He stood on the platform. If he didn't go in he wouldn't be a carrier.

So he wouldn't be a carrier.

He'd back down the ladder, he'd…

Someone pushed him.

He landed face down, put his hands out to break his fall. The heels of his palms pushed forward and he sank, pressing into the soft, rotting bodies.

There was a harness around his shoulders and he felt it heave up.

"Face up!" a voice called down, as if he'd chosen to fall that way. "Twist your head up! Take your fucking pill!"

His legs scrabbled to find purchase but there was none, and he panicked, his throat full of grit and muck, hair across his face, sharpness of bone in his thigh, and he scrabbled, panicked like a child drowning. He screamed but that was worse; a child's hand edged into his mouth and he could taste the last meal, something salt, and he almost blacked out. Another tug on his shoulders roused him.

There was a clear end to the bodies at least. You could stand up and your head would not be submerged. If you tilted your head backwards, mimicking the Man, you could breathe. The bodies had sat there for three weeks at least. Older, many of them and the stench was so powerful McNubbin vomited there and again, couldn't suck new air because his entire self told him he didn't want to breathe it. He stepped up, trying to find purchase, but his heel went through the flesh of a leg, or a stomach, he wasn't sure, but that was a stomach because he could feel the liquid of it, the insides soft and pliable. The press of them against him, the sucking of breath, trying to call for help, trusting that you would be pulled out and you were.

He cried. He forgot about his sugar pill, the one representing an easier death.

"Why did you leave me in there so long?"

"You were in there for two minutes," the instructor said. He was kinder than before; he knew what that pit was like.

You'd never forget it.

McNubbin had recurring nightmares about it, woke up screaming and, his wife said, sweating bitters.

It was enough to haunt you for life and not wish it on your worst enemy. Many a night McNubbin dreamed he went in, or his brother did, in there alive and tap tap tap on the side of the Man, like a code, get me out.

Get me out.

BITTERS

"You're no Timmy Hanlon," his wife said, bringing him back to the present. She squeezed his hands and kissed him. They still felt physical love for each other; was it the bitters that kept things stirring?

They made love quietly that night in their bedroom. It was always so sweet. In the morning though he woke up to see her with tears running down her face. He kissed her awake. "We're still here!" he said. "It's okay."

She tried to sit up.

"Hey, did you find out the joke Thelma told me to tell you? Sorry I'm so dumb."

If she knew he only said those things to give her something to care about, she never let on.

"You are not dumb and you know it! It was nothing. A joke that isn't a joke and that makes it a joke. That's all! She'd be devastated to know it made you feel dumb."

Wanda had a smile on her face now and she threw back to covers to start her day.

＊

They all went to celebrate Hundred Year Day. They took the bus, because the roads were impossible but at least in the bus they could all be together. They went to their local celebration, although as a carrier McNubbin was entitled to the one at the Man.

This one, they got Orton. Looking rich. He always did like the comforts. "Orton's always up at the university. Is he still a professor or what? He sure acts like one," McNubbin's daughter said.

"He's a man who can be in two places at once, I think."

⌐∾⌐

"Every year we stand together to give thanks to those in the Man 100 years hence, because they are who make our bitters today. Those who die young, or die hard. All of them make a difference."

"Hardly scientific," his daughter said.

"You used to talk in words I could understand," McNubbin said, but he kissed her head and he bought little statues for them all.

"How do parents bond with their children without the bitters?" McNubbin said.

Their babies had the stuff mixed with their milk, or soaked in a cloth to suck as they lay in their prams. It calmed them down and built up their immunity. Preventative medicine at its best; you'd find no one to argue against that. Illness rarely came to anyone in the town, not since the plague ran through them two hundred years earlier, but then they were wealthy. They had heated homes, good fresh food. They had exercise grounds, they had good schools. They had every luxury required. It was the perfect place to live.

The one medical doctor in town had an easy job of it. They called him Doctor Cure-all and even he had to laugh at that. Most of his patients were from out of town. Not even the children sickened in the village.

When the professors said, "We need more flu in there, we need some cancer, we need some meningitis or polio," they had to invite the sick to visit. Small doses of each thing and records kept. It was a science. The hospice was second to none in the world and you got in for free if you had the right ailment.

Swain's mother and father had died there. He didn't come from good stock.

Wanda had seen Doctor Cure-all as a patient but it was for other things, not the physical. Sometimes she thought the world would end overnight, and that she was the one responsible. Or she thought that everyone hated her because she never did the right thing.

McNubbin told her (and believed with all his heart) that she was perfect. He told her (and it was true) that he adored her and wouldn't change anything. Sometimes she said that he saved her life on a daily basis. He wondered if she'd still feel this way as a toe-tapper, right there at the forefront doing good. It was hard to say. Doctor Cure-all prescribed her green tea and plenty of green leafy vegetables. He prescribed her a natural sleeping remedy.

You couldn't take anti-depressants and still go into the Man.

Doctor Cure-all called in extra staff for Hundred Year Day. He'd need them; these outsiders came in with colds and other ailments. They sprained their ankles, they fell over, they banged their heads. Every year there were incidents. This year there was a tragedy.

Seventeen hours on the bus, with the chanting, the babies crying, her mother squeezing her hand too hard, too often. "It'll be all right," as if saying it would make Danielle better.

Her mother had the window seat because she liked to look out. Danielle liked the aisle so she could see what was in the bus, what was happening where she was, not elsewhere.

There was no cure ahead, only prevention, but most on the bus chose to ignore that.

The disease spread across them quickly. At first it was the old, the very young and the sick, but before long it was people like Danielle; strong, healthy. She noticed pains in her arms and legs but thought it was muscle ache from exercise (from sex, but she wasn't going to tell her mother that). It didn't lessen, and reports came through of symptoms.

They knew of the Man. Of the bitters. Always had done, had had a small bottle in the medicine cupboard, as most people did. It was disgusting stuff. If the lid was partly unscrewed, you could smell it throughout the house. It smelt a bit like the fermented fish paste her friend Indah used in cooking. Still, they travelled 17 hours to the Man, the source, to be part of the Hundred Year Day, to take the bitters fresh from the Man, to be cured.

Thousands were doing the same. It was a form of religious gathering, really, although most of them wouldn't acknowledge this. A pilgrimage. In other worlds, other towns. Every hotel room booked, every camping place.Every spare room in every house rented out at astronomical costs because this is what kept them going. This is what they did. This was their living.

Many of her fellow passengers were dressed up, as if they were going to a wedding. Some of them wore old clothes on, but they at least wrapped a scarf around, or tried to brighten themselves in one way or another. Most of them were sick. Some of them were dying.

BITTERS

The smell started to seep into the bus an hour or so away from their destination.

It was a shock to those visiting for the first time. Even those who were back again covered their noses, their mouths.

❧

This was Danielle's third visit; her first without her parents.

❧

The radio was tuned to the Hundred Year reading, and the voice calmed her, name after name after name after name after name, of the people they'd be drinking soon and how they'd died. You didn't have to pay attention, but the names were there. You could buy the books of names if you wanted. Families with loved ones in the Man bought them; Danielle had a copy at home.

❧

Across the aisle from her sat Helen, who at 72 was the oldest on board. Danielle sat transfixed as Helen talked about her life, told jokes, made observations. In front of her was Mathias, so handsome he made Danielle speechless. Luckily he was so shy he didn't notice.

On board also, children, other teenagers, parents, lovers, lost souls, loners, dear friends soul mates.

All so hopeful. All buzzing about the Man. How wondrous he was, how kind and benevolent, as if he really existed as an actual person. Danielle had a poster of him on her wall at home and, while she wouldn't admit it to anyone, she did talk to him sometimes about her problems. Especially the guy problems. He never spoke back but she felt that he listened.

Traffic was frantic and she was glad someone else had the responsibility. But then her mother said, "Oh, no," and Danielle could have sworn it was before the bus ploughed into the side of a transport truck. *Fresh Milk*, Danielle could read on the side. The bus and truck ploughed forward, momentum crushing the vehicle and causing the bus to buckle like tinfoil.

This: happened in a split-second.

This: happened forever. Danielle was thrown into the aisle and somehow rolled under Helen's feet. Helen had pillows there, and a quilt, and her spare wool (the knitting she held and the needle pierced her eye, the right one, and her head nodded as if she was sleeping) and it was like some kind of magic under there as the bus rolled.

Danielle heard banging and realized later, bang bang bang bang that was heads against windows, the cracking sounds were heads. Her mother's too, cracked open against the window and nothing to save her.

Mathias stood, was knocked forward (backward), his throat slashed by glass, and he bled so hard all over her she thought she was at home, warm shower, from the time when water didn't hurt her skin.

There was no blessing of unconsciousness.

Her legs were caught but she reached down and tore her pants free. There was no pain.

Around her was just the echo of screams. All else was silent until a beautiful looking man, almost an angel, appeared in the broken window.

He said, "I'm Orton. Let me help." And he reached through the window and helped her out.

Danielle sat in a lush garden. She was bewildered and felt very stupid. He'd told her this was a private hospital and that she'd be looked after. She was weak; she'd been weak a long time now.

"But I need to find Mum."

Her mother. It was possible she survived.

"They're all receiving intensive treatment," Orton said. "Like Cleopatra, bathing in milk, but they are bathing in toetappings."

She wrinkled her nose. Even here, with the Man just a dot in the distance, she could smell him. It was comforting to have him in there. If she was alone, she'd call out to him. Ask him if she should stay or go.

"Best if you wait here," he said. "Until they call for us." He rubbed his finger on his teeth. He did that a lot.

The wine bottle was empty. He assumed she was of drinking age and she didn't tell him otherwise. He led her inside.

He was so good-looking. His skin was beautifully smooth and she felt even more conscious of her measles-pocked face. She hated the sight of herself in the mirror and wondered how he could even look at her. He was a fair bit older but that didn't matter to her. She liked old and young; it all depended on how they carried themselves.

The house was insulated and smelt of an open fire and cinnamon. He brushed his teeth (was it the tenth time?). He was a fair bit taller than her and she found comfort in that, as if he could enclose her in his arms, keep her safe. Heal her. She fancied his skin had a metallic shine but she knew she was dreaming. Delirious.

A small table was set in a sunny corner, and they sat there to eat food that made her feel better. A roasted beetroot salad. An enormous steak with rich sauce. Tiny potatoes cut and shaped to perfect circles.

And more wine.

"What were you hoping for, Danielle?" Orton asked. "In coming here?"

"My mother thought I could be cured."

"And you?"

"I know it's too late. All I have to hope for is a pleasant afterlife. Because this one sucks, to be honest."

"You've enjoyed yourself."

She laughed. "I have! But that's what's so bad. I don't have the energy anymore. Although after that meal…"

"It's nice you have a belief in the afterlife. I don't, myself. I think this is it. That the only thing worthwhile is the Man and what goes into him, what comes out of him. But I'm glad you believe. That must help."

It did, a bit. To believe this wasn't the only chance she'd get.

"So all you've got is the Man, then?"

"All I consider worthwhile. The Man and what goes into him. All my choices have that in mind. I'm about the future of here, not there." He took her hand, caressed it. He said, "This is why I was thrilled to throw your mother in."

"What?"

"She was stiff with fear. She must have been terrified. For you, I bet. More than herself. Did she see the future, do you reckon? Did she know?"

Danielle stood up. His voice had dropped low and he no longer smiled. His whole face drooped as he studied her. "Did she know the terror you would feel as you died? Did she know you'd sound like this?" He opened his mouth and screamed. Her blood-curdled, down to her toes, but that wasn't the worst.

The worst was the other five men who came in when he called.

―――

The bus crash (and three cars as well, jockeying for position on one of the winding roads leading to the Man) meant 48 deaths. 72 injuries to be shipped out.

It was good, once the dead were tested. Privately, the professors rejoiced at the variety that would go into the Man. Mostly they preferred a quiet death, because that way the body wasn't flooded with chemicals.

All that could be done was line the deaths up and work overtime, carry salt carry salt carry salt carry salt bugs until all the death was added to the Man. The professors were pleased; they said the mix would be strong because of it.

This was a crisis time and the town proved itself.

<hr/>

It was supposed to be his day off but McNubbin was called in, along with the rest of the carriers and the salters. Carriers and salters and toe-tappers tended to stick together. There was an understanding of what the job was, which others didn't have.

<hr/>

He kissed his wife goodbye because she didn't want to work that day. "Don't forget you need to look up those girls for me," he said.

"Tomorrow," she said.

He loved her when she was sleepy. He loved her always, but sleepy, he wondered if she was dreaming about him. She'd told him she did; she had erotic dreams where he played a major role. Not that she would let him know the details. She smiled at him sleepily. She was always tired and so was he. A holiday would be nice. *To the mountains, perhaps* she said, because where they lived was so flat you could see a gnat bend over for a shit from a hundred kilometres away.

BITTERS

The first shift back after time off was always hard. Harder on the body each year, McNubbin thought, although he hated to admit his age. It took longer than usual; traffic was worse than ever before. He tried to be patient.

His wife read, "*200 years ago, 100 years since the graveyard filling, we were hit by plague. There can be no doubt of the connection. This was the first definite record of cause and effect. The Man was filled up to pussy's bow then. More came to drink the bitters, and more died, and there he was, spilling out the top.*

"*During the plague, doctors came in, and they made their fortunes (would have made their fortunes) in providing the basic medicine needed for a cure. And all would have gone well, and the town prospered in the bitters.*

"*But we were weaker, and ripe for the picking. It was a hundred years later, 100 years ago, that men with an agenda, a point to prove, and the weaponry to make it happen arrived in town in dozens of transport vehicles, taking all by surprise.*

"*The slaughter, by all reports, was horrendous. The Man shook with the echo of the screams, his toes were lapped with blood. And nothing changed.*

"*Nothing ever changed.*

"*Shifts were doubled then, tripled, depending on what book you read. Carriers up and down the stairs until their skin was soaked through to the bone with sweat. They said the bodies had to be crammed down in order to fit.*

"*One hundred years later, when those victims reached the toe?*

"*The bitters were magnificent.*"

It was McNubbin and his generation who benefited from this. They were the strongest, the healthiest generation the town had seen in some time. And he and others like him took to the carrying like breathing.

***

The queues for toe bitters went for kilometres. Extra stalls were set up; extra licenses given. The visitors bought small carry bags, like mini freezers. The older ones were worth a lot of money these days, if people held onto them. Each bag has a small vial of the bitters, plus a tiny statue of the man, and the book listing the names of the people they would be drinking; those who went into the man a hundred years earlier. At these events in particular, vendors sold small necklaces of the Man. They were cheap reproductions, made in a factory overseas, but they could sell them for a fortune. You screwed off the head and the bitters were inside, and you could keep the Man around your neck at all times if you wanted to.

Everyone received a badge saying "100 Year Day. I love the Man". They walked in clusters, big clumps, only a rare few walking alone. Solidarity, perhaps. Needing to be near each other. McNubbin could understand that. He liked company too.

Talking in quieter tones about the dead people, but all of it *them not us. Their fault not ours.*

Calling for pain killers. Survivors with crutches or whatever, asking for painkillers, and being told, *you won't be allowed in the Man if you take a painkiller. We don't like that in the Man.*

They were tough in the town. Pain was good. Pain was management.

BITTERS

The only thing they really feared was going in the Man alive.

⌐∾⌐

12-hour shifts. Back-breaking work. Carry after carry. Strangers. At least, McNubbin thought, better to die here. Elsewhere you'd be tossed away.

⌐∾⌐

As McNubbin climbed he thought of the fools below. They didn't seem to understand that bitters were preventative, not curative. They queued in a long serpentine line through the town, and fortunes were made selling food and drink, holding places when people needed to shit in one of the many portable toilets lined up like tiny green houses in a miniature suburban street. Money to be made everywhere; selling warm clothing, or newsletters, or books about the Man, selling tickets to things that didn't exist.

⌐∾⌐

McNubbin made his carries quickly. He was in no mood for contemplation. The people at the base annoyed him, clutching at him as if he could provide them with some kind of magical cure. He'd trodden on one child, heard it cry, but you can't look down when you are focused ahead. He didn't kick out, at least, which he was keen to do. Imagine what his wife would say! Imagine Wanda! Always her voice was in his head, *Be gentle*, she'd say. *Be kind*.

McNubbin pushed open the break room door, thinking about a cold glass of beer, perhaps with a drop of bitters to see him through. A shift was exhausting, even on a quiet day when you might only carry one up the stairs. These bus dead were so much more than that.

The lunch room was full of carriers, tappers and salters. All tired. Quiet. But there would be good bonuses, of money and of bitters, once the crowds left.

McNubbin, head bent over his meal in the break room, heard a rise of voices and glanced up. It was Orton, strutting like a peacock, causing a stir as he always did. His shirt was unbuttoned and on his smooth chest sat a small disc, the one professors carried to prove their worth. McNubbin's daughter would have one before long. Orton was barefoot. Clear-eyed, apple-cheeked, but the people of the Man all looked that way. His black hair curly around his face, a studied casualness about him.

The sight of that hair in his eyes annoyed McNubbin. He kept his hair short so it didn't get sweaty and fall over his face. You could never spare a hand for swiping loose hair on a carry. Of course Orton didn't carry. He was the boss.

For a brief moment McNubbin envied his position, and his confidence. They were the same age, yet look at the two of them. Orton lifted weights. McNubbin lifted bodies, carried them, and after 32 years of this he tilted slightly forward. His arm and leg muscles were solid but out of proportion with the rest of his body. Orton was perfectly proportioned.

Orton sat there rubbing bitters into his gums. Licking at it. He loved it as much as anybody else. His skin bursting, he was a big man too big for his skin. Why didn't his skin grow?

And his nails, short below the quick. He didn't age the way McNubbin was aging.

Clive whispered in his ear, "Your cousin got all the looks in the family, didn't he?"

"At least someone in my family does. Your family? Pigs' arses. Anyway he's not my cousin." McNubbin always took the bait on that one, no matter how hard he tried not to.

McNubbin and Orton had been close as kids. They'd built their own man out of plastic, wood, rubbish, built it way out beyond where no one could stop them. They knew it probably wasn't right but they did it anyway. They filled it with dead birds and animals and made a pact to go back in 20 years and see what they'd created.

They never did, though. Life had taken over. Orton a professor and now supervisor, McNubbin out of school at 14 and into the job he was made for.

Orton was elated with the bus crash, although he tried to conceal it. "Sad days," he said. "Sad days indeed, and all we can do is treat them well, and send them to the greatest end known to any civilization." He raised his beer; they all had one, laced with bitters. He'd treated everyone to a fancy lunch, *thank you all*, he said, *and thank you to the dead, too, for giving themselves to the Man. And in such good condition.*

"They're not in good condition," McNubbin said. He didn't often speak up but this was wrong. "They died hard. Like some of the girls we've been taking up. Did you have any thoughts about those young girls?"

Orton blinked at him. "You know that adrenaline is good for the Man, don't you? What goes in must come out. Our population is weaker now than it has ever been. Especially the boys. I'm not wrong. You can't tell me I'm wrong. We have too many suicides. Too many young people dying because of what's missing from the bitters. I'm saving the children a hundred years from now. All of us. We'll be remembered for it."

McNubbin wasn't sure. "But we're all good. We're fine."

"You and I, McNubbin, yes. Because we had the Terror going in. Didn't we? What's coming out now is from the Golden Age, isn't it? When they all died of old age. Peacefully. Good for them, but that's not good for the bitters." He spoke loudly, for them all to hear.

Were the faint cheers genuine or inspired by beer? McNubbin wasn't sure.

Clive came in, soaked the skin, reeking worse than the Man. "Fuck out of here, Clive! You need to shower and change before you get in here. Burn those clothes, mate. Or give them to your servants."

Clive inclined his head. "Not only a broken girl, but drowned also and well past you can even tell she's a girl."

"Not preserved at least?"

"Not even close." He lowered his voice and nodded his head at Orton. "He's the one brought her in. He said she was a bus victim but she wasn't. Does he think we don't know the difference? We know."

"You do the right thing when you take the favours for the professors. They know what they're talking about. That's your job," Orton said. He reached into his pocket and pulled out a wad of bills. "Here, extra. For a new set of clothes. My friend McNubbin is right; you need to burn that lot."

The room was listening now. They always did when the money came out. "I thank you all for your service. Above and beyond. They don't know what you do for them."

He had wine for them all, and more beer, and baskets of food. He'd used his own money, he said, but that didn't mean they owed him anything beyond their dedication to the job.

He was someone who had a voice in the town. He'd saved people from jail. He'd supported marriages and destroyed careers. That was who he was. He had an aura, a magic, and he was a generous man to most. His skin was too tight from too much bitters and his nails too short but people aspired to that. He bought drinks for them all after the shifts ended. And they could also go to him for help. An interest-free loan. A truck to move house. Tiny things only asked in return but McNubbin could see that each of them added up. Each tiny favour added up to a big picture that frightened him. As a professor Orton had many years of education at local University. It was the only school of its kind. Carriers usually leave school at 15. This suited McNubbin very well. It only bothered him when a professor called him stupid and the only one who did that was Orton. They'd teased each other a lot when they were kids, until they didn't anymore.

McNubbin watched him glad-handing around the room, being kindly, CARING, except he cared for nothing.

McNubbin spoke to Orton quietly.

"We're still thinking about these murder victims," he said. He didn't want to waste time with hints. "These young girls coming in broken. Like the one you brought in today. Murder victims."

"That seems harsh. But surely police have cleared them? They have their papers?"

"They're coming in with different records. But we know what they are."

"If they've got their papers then it's nothing to worry about. Not your concern. No need to be prurient."

Then the break was over and they carried, salted, carried, salted, the bus dead. McNubbin carried an older man, who was so light McNubbin could tell his life expectancy had been short. The man's arm hung down over McNubbin's chest and McNubbin could see it was tattooed. An anchor and a love heart and some initials. McNubbin wondered where his great love was. He hoped she'd died on the bus, too, so that they could be together.

It was annoying; he'd have to either slice off the tattoo or cut off the whole arm before putting him in. An extra job and he wouldn't be paid extra for it.

At the top he selected his knife. He cut the whole arm off, because it was a large tattoo, and he threw the limb over the side. He knew the creatures down there would eat it up. Cats, dogs, birds, ants. It'd be gone in a day.

Some people thought animals should go in the man, but the professors were certain that animals would taint the mix, just as bodies preserved did.

"It's not today you will feel the affect, or next year," they said. "But a hundred years from now, the bitters will be tainted. Our reputation will diminish and no one will buy our toe tappings."

BITTERS

Next shift, Swain was back at work, tired and happy. He had a little girl and he showed them photos of a sweet-faced baby with the smear of bitters across her forehead, long, thin fingers grasping a blanket. They'd already decided she'd be a toe-tapper because of those fingers.

"Be good to have one in the family," Clive said. He had two sons who worked as cleaners.

The oldest one was called Clive. Clive often said, "We're all called Clive. They used to number us but they lost track."

McNubbin thought the baby looked pale and too soft, but he didn't say anything.

He rubbed handwax in for protection and set to work. It was the buses still; all those strangers needing carrying.

There was a certain rhythm to it. A disconnection. Usually this was the case, but with an accident like this one, McNubbin found it hard to feel nothing. He carried children, teenagers, adults, very old people. All of them damaged in some way, all of them dead before their time, and that he didn't like.

He carried four, including one he recognized as one of the addicts who slouched around the toes of the Man. His limbs were stiff; he'd been frightened to death, that was clear. It wasn't the first death like that McNubbin seen. Some people loved to scare the shit out of an addict.

Then he rested for a while. They joked around in the break room like they always did, then he had another carry.

This was a young girl, deep facial scars from measles, he guessed. She'd do well in the Man. They needed measles.

But she felt like jelly in his hands. Every one of her fingers was broken, and she was cut head to toe with slashes deep and shallow. Her nose was broken. Her eyes removed. Patches on her head where her hair was torn out. Her hands were covered with defensive wounds, and her arms as well, and her legs.

He paused, holding her.

She was another broken girl.

And he knew that Orton had brought this one in as well.

McNubbin was aches and pains all over and looked forward to a massage from his wife. She did have strong hands no matter how he teased her. He had a deep bath on the way home at the spa, where he caught up with the other workers. Mostly carriers. Somehow the hot steam made the mouths open and they could talk in the semi darkness, about the aches and pains, the bodies they carried, all of it.

They talked about the bus dead, and how it felt to carry a baby up. They talked about how much it all hurt.

No one would touch a pain killer. A tiny drop of toe bitters can ease the pain. The bitters prevented all ills, taken regularly. Diluted in alcohol, poured into bottles. Or the small statues of the Man, people loved those. Replicas of a giant, hand-held, and you could drink straight out of his head if you wanted to. The spout was in his lips so you could put your lips on his and sip away.

Don't drink too much.

It carried warnings that weren't needed. Even the most desperate, the most addicted, could only take so much.

McNubbin stopped the room by calling out about the broken girls and the workers all knew what he meant.

"We need to talk to Orton," one said, but McNubbin shook his head.

"I think it is Orton," he said. "We need to go beyond him." But no one knew what that meant.

McNubbin slept for three hours then was awoken with a call from Clive, his voice full of tears. For all his coolness, he was a feeling man.

"It's Swain's baby. They've had to take her back to the hospital."

"What's happened?"

"They don't know."

"Weakness of the blood," called out the entomologist. Clive must be at the Man. "Look at Swain's parents, died before they were fifty. He won't have a baby lives past one year old."

McNubbin roused Wanda (because she would want to be there for Swain and his wife. That's who she was), but by the time they were washed and dressed word came that the baby was already transferred to the hospice. He couldn't imagine how Swain must be feeling. He knew his parent's great grief when his brother died climbing the steps to the Man's mouth, but that was an adult at least who had lived some life. This was a baby not even begun. Bones still soft.

The children's ward was particularly lovely. Those kids forgot they were sick, they were so happy. And the professors were happy because they knew child bodies carried goodness for the bitters. Newborn babies still held their mother's milk, some of them, and that, in a hundred years, would make for a good drop. You could forget the children were dying when you visited this place. It was so bright and lively. The professors didn't like adrenalin in the mix. They liked endorphins. They liked people to die happy.

Swain and his small family were in a tiny private room. His wife was curled up in a ball, the baby held close to her so you could barely tell body from body. Swain was slumped against the bed, his head on the mattress and his arms crossed as if he was praying to the Man to save them.

Swain said, "It's the weakness of the bitters. Orton is right. It's the professor's fault. It's the fault of the bitters."

A doctor in the room gave a snort, and McNubbin felt such fury towards him he wished he wasn't there. Wanda stepped forward to Swain's wife and held her close. The woman cried so deeply McNubbin couldn't bear to hear it, but he sat with Swain, the four adults in this room, as the baby cooled and all semblance of life was gone.

"I can carry him," McNubbin said. "It would be both and honour and the worst thing I've ever had to do."

"No. I have to," Swain said.

Swain did do it. Clive and McNubbin waited at the foot of the stairs. Clive wanted to go up with him, because they didn't know, they weren't sure. But Swain promised he'd come back down. He wouldn't leave his wife behind.

It was a week later, as the shift neared its end, that McNubbin, Swain and Clive were approached by two security guards from the University.

"Whose turn is it? We've got a favour to ask. One last carry before you go," the taller one said. It was Swain's turn but there was no way. They were all covering for him, who showed up for work because he had to, but couldn't be trusted on the steps.

I'll take it," McNubbin said. They'd share the fee anyway, that's how you managed the extra carries. Even with the sharing, it would be enough for him and his wife to take that holiday they were keen on.

"What'd he die of?" McNubbin asked. He'd take a murder victim up there but not one with the wrong disease. He couldn't do that.

"Longpin to the heart," the men said. They showed him, one small pinprick of blood. It was a big man and the carry would be tough, but McNubbin thought of the money. "And prurience," the other one said. "Orton told us to tell you that."

Clive laughed. "Fucking Orton."

"You got a death certificate?"

Even an unapproved carry needed this.

"Yeah, says heart failure."

"That should be okay," McNubbin said. He'd fudge the time of carry but would never fudge the death certificate. They all knew how important the records were. He didn't feel half as tough as he sounded. He bent over to pick the body up, get it into position. "Hang on," he said. The flesh was soft, almost soggy. Like a sponge. "How old is this death?"

"Only one day. Happened yesterday morning, wasn't it?" and McNubbin understood they were lying, that the death had sat in a freezer for some time. Frozen bodies were a major taboo into the metal giant. There could be no hint of preservation of the body.

It was then he looked at the face, and realized who this was.

It was Jervis, the carrier Swain had replaced, and who had been missing close to a year.

The carrier who refused the extras and who they all thought had given up the Man for life elsewhere.

"Problem?" one of the men said, "Cos if there's a problem, I'm sure we can sort it out with Orton."

"No problem," McNubbin said. He could decide on the way up what to do but one thing he was sure of; he would not allow this body into the Man. He was better than that. For the sake of the Man, and for the sake of Jervis, who believed so completely in the purity of the bitters he had lost his life for it.

"Take him up now. We'll distract the losers around the place."

McNubbin talked to Clive and Swain. He told them about the nature of the death and the length of it, and they were not pleased. He told them it was Jervis.

"It'll be your great great grandchild affected, and mine," Swain said. "You can't put him in." McNubbin had told them about his son expecting and they'd all drunk heartily to that. Then Swain choked; he had forgotten for just a moment he was no longer a father.

"They're showing us Jervis to teach us a lesson. They'll kill us all if you don't do the carry. Stop asking questions," Clive said, his voice cracking. "Bastards. They can't do this to us."

"Orton can do whatever he wants."

Orton affected them all. A man of power and of secrets, he stood like a giant himself, thick-skinned, well-weaponed, protected. McNubbin wondered if he'd have to bend in the middle to fit into the Man.

"What time's your buggy girlfriend coming in?" McNubbin asked, mostly to settle Clive down. Clive checked the charts; two hours.

They were all at the toes of the Man. The toe-tapper said to him, "Don't carry that. You know it's wrong. Follow your instincts. I'll tell them something."

"It'll be all right," McNubbin said.

McNubbin began to trudge to the top.

The sick, weak death of Swaine's baby proved how important the bitters were. How important to get it right.

Once at the Man's head, McNubbin rested the defrosted Jervis against the knife rack and squinted down at the ground, looking for any indication of human movement. He saw none. Funny how the back of the Man was never crowded, as if they were frightened he'd shit on them. At the back corner, behind the giant's left ear, there was an open stretch of land. It wasn't unknown for things to drop down there and this is where McNubbin tipped the body. He knew it would shatter on impact, explode, and there would be little evidence left. He hoped that would suit Orton. At least the body was disposed of.

At the bottom, he saw the stair repairman, deep in embrace with the toe-tapper. McNubbin had forgotten about him. The repairmen were clever with metal, both the stairs and the Man, when the rare split appeared. Cleverness that went back a thousand years and had not been lost.

They nodded at each other; no questions asked.

Travelling home, stuck in traffic that always existed in their busy town, their highly-populated, touristy town, McNubbin worried about the body he'd thrown over. It wasn't the authorities that concerned him; that he could manage. But even if he went to them and explained it himself, he knew that Orton would come out victorious and that McNubbin and his wife, Swain and his family, Clive, they would be the ones to suffer. He had known neighbours and friends destroyed by Orton, often over small perceived slights. McNubbin's conscience was clear, for throwing poor Jervis' unsuitable body over the edge rather than into the Man. He would die pleased that he had done this. But he hoped he would not be caught.

BITTERS

The house was quiet. He hung his work jacket on a chair and set about making dinner. His wife wasn't up yet; she was tired.

McNubbin didn't tell Wanda about the death of Jervis and how he'd dealt with it. She didn't need to know those things. They sat together in the backyard feeling the mosquitoes bite. Passing on the blood, sharing the good stuff. That's what life in this town was all about.

Their son had friends for dinner and their voices rang out, arguing, as young people do. Their son was 16 now and training to be a tapper. They were so proud of him. He wasn't the brightest, or the strongest, but he was a loving kid. His girlfriend already carried a baby for them and that made things set. They all thought about the bitters even more once a grandchild came along about what went in. Because the grandchildren or theirs would be the ones tasting the mix you made.

McNubbin and Wanda exchanged glances.

"We used to have that energy," Wanda said. But McNubbin didn't miss it.

"But if the giant wasn't there. If we closed him up," their son said.

One of his friends said, "I can't imagine. But at least we'd have options."

For McNubbin and Wanda, it didn't bear thinking about. He ended his day weary beyond belief but knowing that he was doing a good thing. He was serving a Man who provided medicine without asking for supplication or sacrifice. All he took were the bodies, and these were worthless elsewhere in the world.

Such precious medicine.

Workers took a small amount per week as part of their pay; it was a major reason why salters, and carriers, and toe-tappers, continued in their work.

Taking a drop of bitters to see you through the rest of the shift. More than a drop and your body would react in strange ways. Many a man had he carried up who'd overused the bitters.

"So tired," Wanda said.

"I did an extra carry today, should see us right for a holiday."

"Somewhere quiet. Away from people always watching us."

"Have you seen anyone?"

"Always seems to be someone watching. Oh. I had Felicity take a look at the records of those girls. All registered. It's a bit worrying they all died of jaundice, though. Is it something going around? What if it takes ours?"

That was no jaundice, he thought. "Ours are fine," he said. But already the sorrow had taken her. She felt it for those girls she'd never even known, and for Swain's baby she'd only seen swaddled and still. She felt it more than he would have thought.

"What is the actual purpose of it all?" she said.

There was no answer to that.

McNubbin made a quick search of the grounds before his next shift, and while there was some evidence of the body, most of it had been eaten by birds, cats, ants. Still, as he entered the break room, he found a security guard there, waiting.

Questions.

McNubbin didn't know the answers he should give, so he told some truth, as much as he could manage. He could not describe the men in detail, but he could describe the body. The weight of it, and how it sat on his shoulder.

"I thought it was official," he said, the main lie he told.

The security guard nodded. "Yes, official. So he should have gone in. Pieces were found, McNubbin. Below. And this is not the way we treat our deaths."

McNubbin shook his head. "I tipped him in."

"You may say that. Well you may. But the powers that be understand the truth as it is, not as you wish it to be." Orton held as much power over this man as he did over everybody else.

Three carries later, he found his wife dead. He knew why she was dead; because he had lost track of her, worrying about Jervis and the broken girls. He'd forgotten how she needed him. Under her side of the bed he found dozens of empty bitter bottles and the worst thought was that someone had forced her to drink them.

No: worst was how willingly she'd gone.

He lay down beside her and breathed deeply; she smelled so beautifully of the bitters, and underneath, her own scent. Tears on his cheeks were thick, viscous. The last time he'd wept was when his father died, and there were tears at the birth of their son, and daughter too, he thought, but those tears were thin, salty.

These were bitter.

Her strength had always astonished him. The power of her love for them all, and the way she got herself up every day when all she wanted to do was sleep.

She had finally given in. He had kept her alive for thousands of days but he couldn't do that forever. Damn Orton for it. Damn him for the guilt, the loss, the pressure.

He heard his son come home and was lost for words. What to say, how to say it? In the end, he called out for him, letting the scene speak for itself. It was weak of him, but honest too, he thought, letting his son parse it for himself.

Seeing his son weeping, McNubbin still did not regret throwing Jervis over the side. For not heeding Orton's warning. Even if his wife was lost; even then. For the good of the bitters, for the future, he knew he'd done the right thing.

He also knew he didn't want to sacrifice his son and daughter to the greater good.

His daughter was at the University. He was thankful she wasn't in the middle of exams. At least that.

He cleaned Wanda up and tidied away the bottles. The police would come but they would do nothing. They were capable of dealing with the small things but never expected to deal with the larger ones.

As they lifted her body they found her last recording. "The end of the history," she had written on it, but all he heard when he played it was, "You can't make me stay any longer. Why did you make me stay so long?" And when he pulled on his work jacket, he saw that she had picked the stitches from the tiny pocket and taken his pill.

His daughter came in. His son had told her, for which McNubbin would be forever grateful. She fell to her knees, holding her mother's hand. No tears, yet.

"Why would she leave us?"

"I need her. My baby's going to need her," his son said. All of them stunned at this.

"What made her do it? And where did she get it all?"

He loved his children for never imagining he gave her the bitters. He never would; they'd lived under the same rules as everybody else. The same restrictions in amounts.

"I think it was my pill she took. I left it there, in my jacket, where she could get hold of it, and I never noticed."

He wished the two of them were still young. Childhood is slow and steady. No moments of great joy, no moments of great sorrow. It's only when you have your own family, or when you make your lifelong friends, that true sorrow or joy can be felt. He thought if he'd let her die then? If he hadn't kept her alive, they wouldn't feel it so strongly now.

But that was wrong and he knew it. Every minute they'd had was worthwhile.

※

The feel of his wife's breasts was no different to any other woman he had carried up the stairs, but these ones he knew the taste of. The perfumed sweetness when they first met. The other sweetness, of the bitters she used when pregnant, to toughen and prepare her nipples for the baby. The sweetness of her milk that time he pushed his infant's daughter's feet aside to suck at her free breast and she had laughed so hard father and baby were shaken off.

He shifted his wife gently to his other shoulder. He had felt her weight on him when they made love, many times. They were magic together and he would never be with another woman. He had no desire for anything but his memories.

Below, two toe-tappers began their work. Was there a slight gurgle? The Man was always digesting.

He spoke softly to her as he walked, all the things he would have told her had she been alive. About his day, and who he'd carried, and how Swain's wife was, and the crazy things Clive said. He wanted to hear her talk of the files, give him the details of illnesses and pain, the way she always did, and the tears that came threatened to unbalance him.

Still he climbed.

There was the buzz and gentle tapping of a million insects inside the Man.

He reached the top. He cleaned the knife against his shirt, and drew it across her throat. There was no blood there, just an ooze of something clear and almost solid. He wiped her brow and kissed it. He said, "Give thanks that in one hundred years you will nourish a child," and he tipped her into the Man's head.

He trudged back down again, desperately lonely, knowing that she would not be at home for him.

BITTERS

When he got down, Orton was at the toe, scavenging drops as he loved to do, nudging Thelma the toe-tapper as she worked, making out she was sexy. McNubbin thought, *He's going to sack me. It must be as important as that for him to come for me like this.*

"I'm so sorry for your loss, McNubbin. It's a terrible, terrible thing. At least you've been loved, though. You're lucky in that."

McNubbin let the tears fall, then.

"I wanted to talk to you alone, McNubbin. Because I know you'll understand. I know we think the same way."

"Why am I carrying so many girls that have been beaten to death, Orton?" McNubbin said. He didn't care who heard it.

"These are good girls. Doing good for the Man. Adding adrenaline. You're the one who alerted me to this. Don't you remember? Telling me you know the difference between those who died in fear and those who died in peace."

"You never listen to me," McNubbin said, pleased despite himself. At the same time he recognized the role he had played in causing the deaths of the girls through his statement. He was showing off. Trying to prove he was smart.

"You know this is common practice. We always manipulate what goes into the Man."

Orton's voice so gentle, yet bruises on his knuckles. Scratches on his forearms.

"The professors don't agree with you about what goes in," McNubbin said. "That's why you're here now. Not there. You aren't always right."

"Oh, but I am, you know."

Orton stood over him and McNubbin suddenly, stupidly, understood the extent of his power. "I came to invite you along. You understand about the girls. The fear. I've come to invite you along to the next one. To share."

McNubbin reacted instinctively, pushing Orton backwards. His arms, his shoulders, very strong. The toe-tapper (it was Thelma) stood to protect her bottles, but at the same time covered her eyes deliberately: *I can't see a thing*, she was telling him. *You go for it.*

So Orton hadn't changed. It wasn't about the bitters. Not only, anyway.

"You're pure evil. I'm not like that."

"I would have taken your sister if she'd been capable of feeling anything. I could have loved that one. Your daughter would be worthy. We'll be watching you. The system only works if we all believe in it. Us, and our families. Our wives. Only what way will we survive. No more questions, McNubbin. Let's be clear on that."

"I will be asking," McNubbin said. "You watch."

"There are more to come," Orton said. "Your wife is already bitters, and so is your son. Your daughter. And the baby on the way. Already bitters."

McNubbin said, "We will carry no more broken girls. We will not."

"You will, or you will be bitters."

"We are all bitters in the end," McNubbin said.

Orton took a bottle of the bitters and walked away. McNubbin felt shaken by the encounter, unsure of what to do.

"He's rotten," Thelma said. "You stick to your guns. Whatever we can do to help, we will."

"What if he's right?"

"There's not one of us who'd like to see the bitters improved on the suffering of others. Not one. And that man, he loves the suffering for the sake of it. I reckon he hangs out down here to see the misery."

They watched the addicts and it was true; what you saw was pure misery.

At the toe, Thelma gave him a hug. She'd been crying, because Wanda was a dear friend and she'd help keep her alive, too. "Listen," she said. "I'm with you. You can't take any more of the broken ones. That's what broke Wanda in the end. Knowing that these things are in the world. That babies can die, and girls are killed unnoticed. We have failed so badly."

Clive and Swain waited for him in the break room. Clive made them strong bitter tea, sweetened with too much sugar, and they sat together and talked about his loss. There were no secrets amongst those who climbed the stairs. You were laid bare each time.

They had done the same for Swain and the two men wept while Clive wiped his own tears of sympathy away.

Then Orton, again. Not leaving a minute, not giving a moment. He said, "We don't care how we get our message across and the message is this: sometimes we need help and you are the men to help us. This town functions smoothly because of our machinations. I need to show you something, McNubbin."

They travelled back to their childhood suburb, a short journey. Then out to the far reaches, where the land was still barren and empty.

"I'm sorry about your wife," Orton said. "That shouldn't have happened."

McNubbin didn't answer. They walked out into the centre, where the man they'd built lay.

It was a disgusting heap of wood, plastic, and bones. They used to argue about what went in. McNubbin had wanted to put the animals in dead. Only the ones they found that way. But Orton wanted to hunt the animals, kill them, put them in.

That's who he really was. McNubbin never forgot that.

There was the faint hint of decay, but nothing compared to what they were used to.

"Decay is good. Vital for survival," Orton said, standing legs apart over their rotted man. "Entropy is important. This is what we had together. When we worked together. And now we are on our own again. Just the two of us."

"We used to argue. You wanted them to die hard. Even then."

"Yeah. I did."

"Why destroy them so completely?"

"I've told you. For the adrenaline."

"My daughter says no. Most agree adrenaline is not good. It affects other elements. Negates them."

Orton said, "A woman would say that. They're the ones who benefit without it. It's the boys I'm worried about."

McNubbin's son was gentle. His girlfriend was the strong one. "There's nothing wrong with that." Orton gave him a look of scorn. "Addicts, the lot of them. You're one of the good ones. You deserve greatness. The ones who can't take it don't deserve to have it. They make a mockery of it all, turn the bitters into an addiction rather than something pure and beautiful." But there was plenty of talk of Orton and how he couldn't leave it alone.

"I'm offering a disposal service. We honour those who died by giving them a place in the man," Orton said. "It is a great privelege."

"The service is to the people who broke them, not for anyone else." McNubbin said. He could hardly bear to be here with Orton. How was it that others adored him? Listened to him?

"You and I agree on the weakness of this generation. Don't we?"

McNubbin shook his head, but that was a lie. He found them irritating, most of the young people. Lazy, uninformed, and, yes, weak.

"Why now?" McNubbin said. "And why are they dying that way?"

Orton said, "Sad and all. Very sad. But at the same time... it was you, McNubbin. Showing your smarts, talking about your observations of those who'd died in fear. How rare that is, and what a difference it makes to the way the body feels. We're not scared enough anymore. We don't feel anything.

The bitters needs adrenalin. Our boys are weakening and it's because of the mix."

McNubbin had to agree. Of his children's generation, the girls were the strong ones. The smart ones. His daughter was stronger and smarter than his son and that was for sure. Though his son had managed to get his girlfriend pregnant, and she was a good young woman, someone he'd be proud to have in the family, so no saying he was a failed child.

He realized that beyond his disgust at the way the broken girls died, he was surprised. He couldn't imagine his daughter and her friends as victims. They were too strong; they were too confident.

"We need to help the boys be strong again," Orton said. "You know I'm right," Orton said to him, only him. "You know we are ripe for destruction unless we take action."

Even a quiet mouse stirs.

Evil starts quiet, sometimes. A show of greed as a child, an unwillingness to share. Clarity in a group, when others work together and this one works alone, yet this one is rewarded.

McNubbin said to Orton, "Thelma the toe-tapper wants to see you," and he winked. At their age there wasn't much of that, and she was sweet, Thelma, and toe-tappers are known for the juiciness of their lady parts. "She's lovely," McNubbin said, making it worse. "I've always had a quick go before heading up or coming down. She's up for it and she's asked for you."

BITTERS

Orton was thrown by this, not what he expected, and he followed McNubbin, quiet for a change. Rumour was his wives had left him for failure to perform. Perhaps he thought Thelma would wreak magic on him.

She waited, pressed against the right heel of the Man. It was shadows under there, and it smelt of cold places, but McNubbin could see Thelma, her shirt down off her shoulders, her breasts white and so smooth.

"You came," she said, and she reached for Orton. She stroked his hair, tilting his head back, and somehow he allowed it; somehow he let her be in control. She lifted a bottle of Bitters and Bubbles, a town favourite, and she poured some directly into his mouth.

The drug took effect within minutes. It was Wanda's leftover sleep medication. She'd wake up bright as a button after a night on this.

"Are we sure?" McNubbin said. Thelma nodded. "It's for Wanda, and for all the broken girls," he said, as if she needed convincing. It was more for himself; proving that he was right in this.

McNubbin had asked Felicity, his wife's best friend at the archives to check the medical records. Orton was a perfect addition; cured case of venereal disease, childhood measles.

"Wanda always did say you were a softy," Felicity had said when they met. She rubbed his arm and seemed to purr. McNubbin felt such deep revulsion his stomach ached.

"You shouldn't," he said, but she didn't seem abashed.

He wished she wasn't there. He'd ask someone else for help with files next time. They all liked him at the Archives.

✦

Clive, Swain and McNubbin carried two bodies at a time for the shift, Clive even taking three in one carry because one was a child and the other an emaciated old woman.

This saved them the hour needed.

They stripped Orton naked because nothing but flesh goes in. With his shoes off, he was so much shorter. McNubbin laughed. "Look at him! Great big lifts in his shoes!" and the three of them laughed till they wept.

They tied Orton up, wrapping him like a mummy to make him easy to carry.

Orton was lighter than he looked, as if he had no soul and was merely a husk. Every step, McNubbin thought of his wife, and of all this man did to control the town. How little he did to benefit the citizens, and how well they would do without him. There was no hesitation.

✦

There were a lot of steps.

✦

At the top he propped him as he had propped so many before. He unwrapped the bandages, leaving Orton pale and thin and naked.

BITTERS

After ten minutes, Orton began to stir. The stench at the top was so powerful, no person could sleep through it. McNubbin lifted him up by his armpits and folded him so that his back bent over into the skull, his feet lifting off the ground.

"What?" Orton said. Sleepy, befuddled. He was not used to being out of control; this hadn't happened since he was eight years old.

"You're at the top. You're here. You're a lucky man," McNubbin said. He hoisted Orton's knees. "You know who I am? I am McNubbin. Husband of the woman you killed. I represent all the husbands, all the wives. All the broken girls and the future generations, the damage you do to the bitters, not caring who goes in."

"No!" Orton said. McNubbin lifted him by the ankles, dangled him in.

McNubbin said, "You are smarter but I am stronger. You won't find a stronger man than a carrier. They say you could survive for a week in there. There's food. There's liquid to drink. Who knows?"

Orton wriggled like a fish, jerking insanely, as if all control of his body was gone. He screamed, a high-pitched hysterical scream. Incapable of speech, incapable of lifting himself forward, he screamed as if to burst his own eardrums, die from it.

"Adding adrenaline now," McNubbin said. Orton stopped screaming as McNubbin spoke. "You always said you wanted to be remembered. Well, you will. In secret, anyway. As the second person to fall in the Man alive."

McNubbin dropped him.

Bending over, holding tightly to the side, he could hear a slight thump, a squelch, and the muffled sound of Orton's screaming.

He began the long walk down, each step accompanied by the gurgles, the buzzes and the squeaks of the Man digesting.

CEMETERY DANCE PUBLICATIONS
PAPERBACKS AND EBOOKS!

DEAR DIARY: RUN LIKE HELL
by James A. Moore

DEAR DIARY:
Run Like Hell
JAMES A. MOORE

Sooner or later even the best prepared hitman is going to run out of bullets. Buddy Fisk has two new jobs, bring back a few stolen books of sorcery, and then stop the unkillable man who wants to see him dead...

"Gripping, horrific, and unique, James Moore continues to be a winner, whatever genre he's writing in. Well worth your time."
—Seanan McGuire, *New York Times* bestselling author of the *InCryptid* and *Toby Daye* series

DEVIL'S CREEK
by Todd Keisling

DEVIL'S
CREEK
A NOVEL
TODD
KEISLING

When his grandmother Imogene dies, Jack Tremly returns to his hometown to settle her estate. What he finds waiting for him are dark secrets which can no longer stay buried.

"Keisling skillfully evokes the landscape and inhabitants of south-central Kentucky, as well as the struggles of his protagonist to deal with a past resurgent in the most immediate and frightening ways. Another step forward for him, Devil's Creek shows why Todd Keisling runs at the front of the pack."
—John Langan, author of *Sefira and Other Betrayals*

GOTHIC
by Philip Fracassi

PHILIP
FRACASSI
GOTHIC

A famous but struggling horror writer. A mysterious antique desk with an otherworldly origin. A woman who will stop at nothing to retrieve it. When Tyson Parks receives the desk as a gift, his long-lost inspiration returns, revitalizing his career. The desk's gifts aren't free, however. They demand a price. One Tyson may be all too willing to pay…even if it's his sanity, and the ones he loves most.

"A diabolical novel! Fracassi pens this one with furious, devilish glee. Readers—and writers—of horror fiction will love it."
—Ronald Malfi, author of *Black Mouth*

Purchase these and other fine works of horror from CemeteryDance Publications today!
www.cemeterydance.com

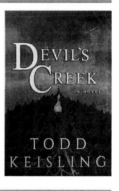